Jac
Little Party

BOB GRAHAM

**WALKER
BOOKS**

For Esme
and her collie dog, Bowsprit

First published 2007 by Walker Books Ltd
87 Vauxhall Walk, London SE11 5HJ

4 6 8 10 9 7 5 3

This book has been typeset in Bembo Educational
and BobGraham

Printed and bound in China

British Library Cataloguing in Publication Data:
a catalogue record for this book is available from the British Library

ISBN: 978-1-4063-0664-4

www.walker.co.uk

School's Out

5

The Grooblies

25

The Party

43

School's Out

"Happy Birthday, Jack!" his mum
called. Jack was embarrassed by his mum
– specially wheeling that old pram, with
Madam Brown the guinea pig inside and
his little brother Duggie perched on top.

Jack's mum was not like the other
mums. "Hi, Jack!" she called.
Jack pretended
not to hear.

He made a neat little sidestep around
Mum's kiss and turned it into a game
of football with his friend Sam.

Sam was coming home with Jack
this afternoon for Jack's
birthday tea.

Just the two of them
(not counting Duggie
and Madam Brown).

"Mum, why did you have to bring that old pram? Why not the low racy one with three wheels?" Jack asked.

"Because Madam Brown's cage won't fit. And you know Duggie won't come without her," replied Mum.

Jack did know really.

12

"Nice you could come home for Jack's birthday, Sam," said Mum.

"Thanks, Mrs Bell," replied Sam.

"I've got a little party all ready, but first we're going to stop by Paradise Gardens," said Mum.

In the shopping centre Mum took them to have their photos taken.

"Just to remember your special afternoon," she said. A blind rolled down behind them.

"Oh, it's just like you're in the countryside," Mum laughed.

CHILD
PORTRAITS

The camera flashed and she
bought two prints.

"Sam's mum and dad have a
digital camera so you can see
your own pictures on the
computer," said Jack.

Mum put the photos safely away
behind Madam Brown's cage.

In the video games parlour right opposite, Jack and Sam played Green Slime Two.

"You two boys look really serious," said Mum. "Only your thumbs are happy and dancing." And she laughed.

Then Mum played a game with
Duggie. His little fat finger poked at
the buttons at all the wrong times.

But each time he outran the Slime.

"It's a miracle!" Mum laughed again
and kissed his finger.

"Your mum laughs a lot," whispered
Sam.

On the way home, Mum said,
"Jack, didn't you go to Sam's for a
party last year?"

"Yes, he's got this massive house …"
Jack kicked a stone. "…and there were
lots of kids there, and a cool magician,
and a Quest Treasure Hunt – oh!
and there was a DJ too, and we all
won mini radios."

"I bet they didn't play 'I Spy'," said
Mum.

"Oh, Mum," replied Jack.

But Mum continued, "I spy with my little eye …"

"Mum… Duggie can't spell," said Jack.

"…something beginning with … GREEN." And she looked right at a weed growing through the crack in the path. Then she looked at Duggie.

"Bicks!" yelled Duggie.

"What's BIX?" said Sam.

"He means 'bricks',"
said Mum, "he can't say his 'r's yet."

"And bricks are red. He doesn't
get it," said Jack.

Duggie's bottom lip jutted out.

"Well he can
sure beat the
Green Slime,"
said Mum,
"and you two
with your tricky
little thumbs
got Slimed."

They rounded the last corner.

"Well here we are, and it's something beginning with H," said Mum.

"Home!" everyone yelled (everyone except Duggie and Madam Brown).

On the balcony, held by
pegs on the washing line, was a poster:
"HAPPY BIRTHDAY JACK"

"Your dad won't be home yet."
Mum put the key in the lock but
then stopped. "Do you want to play
The Grooblies?"

The Grooblies

"No, Mum, that's a dumb game."

Jack scrubbed at a spot with his toe.

"What's The Grooblies?" asked Sam.

"Nothing," replied Jack.

"Well it has to be *something*," his friend said impatiently.

"It's … it's … for little kids."

"Let's play it with Duggie
then," said Sam.

Duggie
brightened up.

Jack worked
on his spot
a little more,
then said,
"Well, it
was a game
when I was young…"

"And I would say
to Jack," Mum continued, "'Jack,
if you don't get your pyjamas on
by the time I count to ten …
the Grooblies will get yer.'"

"And sometimes Mum
only got to three, and
I would get excited…
I mean *really* excited,"
said Jack.

"AND?" Sam asked.

"And I would dive into bed
as fast as I could," Jack answered.

A jet passed high overhead,
so high it made no sound.

Mum broke the silence.
"Sometimes the Grooblies got
him," she said.

"Mum would pin my arms to
my sides and tickle me, or worse
still … leave a big lipstick mouth
mark on my face, or something,"
said Jack.

31

Mum hunched her shoulders.
Her voice went throaty. "The Grooblies
will get yer," she whispered,
low and menacing.

Jack looked
at Sam.
Sam looked
at Jack.

32

No one looked at Duggie.
Duggie ran.

Mum held her arms out and she curled
her fingers. *Clomp! Clomp! Clomp!*
She came slowly forward…

"Mum, don't … don't be … Mum …
NO!" said Jack. But the boots
kept coming.

Sam laughed
nervously. Then he turned – his
sneakers squealing on the concrete – and
he was gone, with Jack close behind.
Duggie was way out in front, running as
fast as his little legs could take him.

Clomp! Clomp! Clomp! Mum's boots came closer and closer.

The laughs turned to shrieks

of excitement, and as the boys passed Duggie, his lip started to quiver.

"Don't worry, love, you can be a Grooblie," said Mum scooping him up under one arm, like a very large handbag.

Round and round they went. The
noise bounced off the high brick walls.

"Don't get Groobled!" yelled Sam.
"Not this time!" shouted Jack.

Mum was close behind, but rapidly
slowing into a lopsided rolling
walk with the weight
of the smaller
Grooblie swinging
off her. Duggie hung,
waved his arms and
watched the ground
come to a stop
underneath.

A window flew up. It was the cross
lady from upstairs.

"If I've told you children once about
making a noise in the courtyard, I've
told you a—"

Then she stopped.

She saw Jack's mum, puffed and red
and laughing. She saw a small child
slipping slowly to the ground.

"I'm sorry, we were … er … we
were …" said Mum.

The cross lady's mouth went very thin
– then the window slammed down.

"…having fun," said Mum.

As they climbed the stairs, Sam said,
"That was more fun than a Quest
Treasure Hunt."

"I guess it was," Jack replied.

"Bicks," said Duggie, and pointed to
the wall.

"See? He does get it," said Sam. "But
Duggie, they're red, not green."

"Perhaps we should start Jack's little
party," Mum said, and once more
put the key in the door.

The Party

On the table were three chocolate frogs in ponds of green jelly (two had their heads bitten off already by Duggie).

There were hot sausage rolls, and a fat snowman, a green marshmallow snail, a chocolate seal, a blue meringue bird and some apple for Madam Brown.

There was also a plate of peanut-butter sandwiches which probably no one would eat.

Dad came home at the end of the party.
He kissed Mum.
Then he kissed Duggie. Then he tried
to kiss Jack.

For the second time that day, Jack ducked.

Dad made a pretend punch, like dads sometimes do.

"Having a good birthday, Jack?" he said.

"OK," replied Jack.

There was nothing left to eat so Dad
had the peanut-butter sandwiches.

"I remember you, Sam," said Dad.
"You had the party on the hill. With
the magician," he added.

"And he had a huge birthday cake,"
said Jack, "specially from the shop,
with a big windmill on top – and sails
that turned around. All made out of
little coloured Smarties," he said.

"Well, speaking of cakes, I've got a little something to finish with," said Mum. She went into the kitchen.

Duggie slurped the last of his red drink.

Dad blew a wizzer, which quickly
uncurled and stopped
just short of the
guinea pig.

"You're frightening
Madam Brown,"
said Jack.
"Sorry!" replied Dad.

Then Mum returned
with the cake.

"I made it myself," said
Mum. "It's a bit lopsided."

It was a Great White Shark with a wide open red mouth. It burst up through a sea of grey icing, some of which still dripped from the plate.

"AWESOME," yelled Sam. "Teeth and everything!"

"Well thank you, Sam," replied Mum and shook some icing from her hair.

A candle perched right on top of the
shark's nose.

Jack had just blown it out when
a knock came at the door.

It was Sam's mum, but she got two
phone calls before she could talk.

"Sorry. Busy, busy," she said.

"Mum, did you bring the present?"
asked Sam.

"I ... er ... no, Sam, I'm sorry."

"Oh, MUM!"
said Sam.
"Well, it
was a new
game on
PlayStation,"
he said. "Tank
Trap Three."

"Um … well, next time
I'm at your house
we can play it
there," said Jack.

Then Sam's mum
said, "Thank Jack's
mother for having
you, Samuel."

"Thank you," said Sam.

"It was a pleasure, Sam, come again," said Jack's mum. She handed him a photo in an envelope and a huge piece of shark to take home, and said, "There are nice chunks of icing in there too, Sam."

"Thank you, must fly," said Sam's mum, and just before Sam was whisked away he leant close to Jack and said, "I think your mum's GREAT."

And Jack said, "Yes, she is."

Then they were gone into the traffic.

"Jack, you didn't tell Sam we don't have a PlayStation," said Mum.

"No," said Jack, "it would have been too sad for him if I couldn't use his present."

There was silence.

Then Jack said, "Mum, at least you don't say to me 'Say thank you' when we're leaving parties."

"I'm sure you would say it all by yourself, Jack," she answered.

That night, while Madam Brown
kept Duggie company in his cot,
Jack read a note pinned to his
bedroom door.

Jack thought he was too old for this
sort of thing ... but he made it in time,
clothes and all.

And he got a big kiss mark
anyway, right in the
middle of his forehead.